DANDELIONS

EVE BUNTING

DANDELIONS

Illustrated by
GREG SHED

HARCOURT BRACE & COMPANY
San Diego   New York   London

Requests for permission to make copies of any part of the
work should be mailed to: Permissions Department,
Harcourt Brace & Company, 6277 Sea Harbor Drive,
Orlando, Florida 32887-6777.

Library of Congress Cataloging-in-Publication Data
Bunting, Eve, 1928–
Dandelions/Eve Bunting; illustrated by Greg Shed. — 1st ed.
p.   cm.
Summary: Zoe and her family find strength in each other
as they make a new home in the Nebraska territory.
ISBN 0-15-200050-X
[1. Frontier and pioneer life — Nebraska — Fiction.
2. Family life — Nebraska — Fiction.
3. Nebraska — Fiction.] I. Shed, Greg, ill. II. Title.
PZ7.B91527Dan   1995
[Fic] — dc20   94-27104

First edition
A B C D E

Printed in Singapore

The paintings in this book were done in
designer gouache on canvas.
The display type was set in Goudy Open Italic
by Solotype, Oakland, California.
The text type was set in Goudy Old Style
by Thompson Type, San Diego, California.
Color separations by Bright Arts, Ltd., Singapore
Printed and bound by Tien Wah Press, Singapore
This book was printed with soya-based inks on
Leykam recycled paper, which contains more than
20 percent postconsumer waste and has a
total recycled content of at least 50 percent.
Production supervision by Warren Wallerstein
and Ginger Boyer
Designed by Kaelin Chappell

To the librarians and teachers of Nebraska,
with special thanks to James E. Potter, historian,
Nebraska State Historical Society,
for his help.
—E. B.

To Lila and Jim, my parents,
and to Sharon, my wife, whose love and support
made this possible. With thanks to Hoyt,
Katie, and Stephanie.
—G. S.

We came to Nebraska Territory in the spring.

Our oxen, Brownie and Blackie, pulled the wagon and our cow, Moo, was tied on behind.

It was a long way from my grandparents' home in Illinois. A long, long way.

Papa laughed and sang. "Look at it, Emma," he said to Mama. "Miles and miles of free land."

"But it's so lonely . . . ," Mama said.

"We won't be lonely," Papa promised. "We have each other and the girls, and in the fall there will be the new baby." His voice sounded almost holy. "A new baby in a new land."

My little sister, Rebecca, put her mouth close to my ear. "Where are the trees, Zoe?"

"We'll come to some," I said.

We did. But not many.

Day after day we trundled along, our wagon wheels making their own tracks through the tall grass.

"See how the grass closes behind us?" Mama asked. "It's as if we'd never been."

We cooked our meals outside the wagon and slept on Mama's quilts spread on the ground. Papa told us the names of the stars and about the moon, how it rose and set, and how the moon and the stars were the same ones that shone over Grandma and Grandpa's house. The very ones we used to see through our bedroom window.

When he told us that I cried a little, but I didn't let Rebecca see.

The sound of the wind in the grass was like the sound of the rivers we'd known back home. Day and night the sound was in our ears.

Sometimes we came to real rivers, and when we did we washed ourselves and topped up our water kegs. Sometimes a river was easy to cross and sometimes hard, with Brownie and Blackie so frightened as they swam, and us holding on to them and to the wagon, too. Sometimes we even had to cross on a ferry pulled by ropes.

It had been weeks since we started our journey. Twelve miles a day, if we were lucky. One day we did seventeen.

It was late summer now and scorching hot from red sunrise to red sunset.

Our supplies were running low.

Mama had a birthday, and we used the last of the flour to make johnnycakes. They were the best I'd ever tasted.

One day Papa said, "Mama and I have talked things over. I must take the wagon into town and stock up. Zoe will come with me. Rebecca and Mama will come as far as the Svensons'. They can have a nice visit there till we get back."

"But I want to go to town, too!" Rebecca screamed. "It's not fair. I don't want to stay with those horrible Svenson boys." Rebecca doesn't scream often. But not going to town was something to scream about.

"You will come next time," Papa promised her. "It is too far and too hot for Mama to make the trip. Mrs. Svenson understands about babies being born, and Mama will be safe there. Zoe is older and can be a help to me. You must be a help to Mama."

There was no more to be said.

I was very excited, but I tried not to show it because it would make Rebecca feel worse.

It took a lot of preparation but at last we were on our way with Moo tied behind us so she could be milked at the Svensons' and so she wouldn't be lonely while we were gone.

Our neighbors were glad to see us again. They made a list of things they wanted us to bring back for them, and soon Papa and I were off, our water kegs refilled to the tip-top.

"Matthew? Are you sure you can find your way back?" Mama called, running heavily after the wagon. "Can you mark your trail?"

"With bread crumbs?" Papa asked, smiling. "Try not to worry, Emma. We will be fine."

He and I were both quiet, knowing she would worry anyway.

At last Papa said, "There is a little extra money. We will get something pretty for Mama to mark her birthday. You can help me choose."